W9-CED-827

KATIE DAVIS

I'm telling you, Dex, Kindergarten Rocks!

VOYAGER BOOKS

HARCOURT, INC. • Orlando Austin New York San Diego London

I am Dexter Dugan and I know everything about kindergarten. This is because I am actually going to *be* a kindergartner.
Very soon.

I am an expert because my big sister, Jessie, went there too one time.

My dog Rufus is an eensy teensy beensy bit scared about kindergarten.

Jessie went to kindergarten a long, long, long, long, long, long, long, long, long, long, long time ago (but she still remembers it even though she's going into third grade).

When Jes went to kindergarten, she wasn't big like she is now.

She wrote like me. And she drew like me, too.

Only not as good.

I got Jessie to help me make a list of things Rufus was scared about.

I'm not worried though.

Kindergarten will be
a piece of cake.

Nooooo problem.

I can't wait.

When the bus came the next morning,
the driver seemed like he knew what he was doing, so I got on.

Rufus was still worried, but Jessie had a great idea.

When we finally got to school, I couldn't wait to see my classroom.

There are some *kind of* good surprises about kindergarten.

For one thing, my friend Joey from preschool was there.
Rufus was so happy to see him, he forgot to worry.

We made art,

I think Rufus wants to lick the spoon.

and cooked food,

and smushed Play-Doh.

I got to write letters,

and build a gigantic tower,

and play in the
imagination station,

and look at books.

Then we went to the library. That's where you go if you want to know about snails or soccer or outer space or shark guts. You can borrow a whole book all about it and keep it practically forever.

At lunch you get to eat with all your friends in the cafeteria.
It's exactly almost like a restaurant.

And there are people called custodians who clean the whole entire school
and they help you even when you spill your milk by accident
and you are scared you'll get in trouble.

After lunch, everyone goes to recess. Joey says you can't get lost playing
I-Am-A-Monster-And-You-Are-A-Powerful-Monster-Getter
because if someone's always chasing you, how can you get lost?

Rufus was so happy to see me. He knew I'd find him the whole time.

I'm going to learn lots of stuff in kindergarten,
but the thing I learned today was . . .

To my former teachers Mrs. Cook, Mr. Saunders, and Mrs. Ciricillo;
to the fabulous teachers at my kids' school;
to all teachers who inspire and ignite our children every day
— K. D.

Special thanks to:
My children, Benny and Ruby, who let me use their artwork in the book.
Another to Ruby, who, based on her own kindergarten experience, came up with the title.
And Ms. Sugarman, for being an enthusiastic listener, guide, and model, and who is as sweet as her name.

Copyright © 2005 by Katie Davis

All rights reserved. No part of this publication may be reproduced or transmitted in any form or by any means, electronic or mechanical, including photocopy, recording, or any information storage and retrieval system, without permission in writing from the publisher. For information about permission to reproduce selections from this book, please write Permissions, Houghton Mifflin Harcourt Publishing Company, 215 Park Avenue South, NY, NY 10003.
www.hmhbooks.com

First Voyager Books edition 2008

Voyager Books is a trademark of Harcourt, Inc., registered in the United States of America and/or other jurisdictions.

The Library of Congress has cataloged the hardcover edition as follows:
Davis, Katie (Katie I.)
Kindergarten rocks!/written and illustrated by Katie Davis.
p.   cm.
Summary: Dexter knows everything there is to know about kindergarten and is not at all scared about his first day there, but his stuffed dog, Rufus, is very nervous.
[1. First day of school—Fiction.
 2. Kindergarten—Fiction.
 3. Schools—Fiction.]
I. Title.
PZ7.D2944Ki   2005
[E]—dc22   2003022623
ISBN 978-0-15-204932-4
ISBN 978-0-15-206468-6 pb

SCP   15 14 13 12 11
4500434162

The display type was set in Lemonade Bold.
The text type was set in Elroy.
Color separations by Bright Arts Ltd., Hong Kong
Printed in China by RR Donnelley, China
Production supervision by Christine Witnik
Designed by Linda Lockowitz